LUTHER IS AWESOME!

GREta ROCKS!

Michael Wayne (signature)

FUNNY SHORTS

SHORT STORIES
THAT MAKE KIDS LAUGH
(and adults
shake their heads)

written by
Michael
Wayne

illustrated by
Jeremy
Manning

For Tricia.
Who enjoys
when I laugh
at my own jokes.
–Michael–

For Mom.
I'm not bored anymore.
I finally went
and drew something.
–Jeremy–

First Edition 2020
Shorty Pants Books
www.shortypantsbooks.com

ISBN: 978-1-946976-07-9
Printed in Canada

FUNNY SHORTS

PIRATE AT THE PET STORE

Avast, how do you like me new parrot?

That's not a parrot. It's a flamingo.

Arrr!

Avast, how do you like me new parrot?

That's not a parrot. It's a monkey.

Arrr!

Avast, how do you like me new parrot?

That's not a parrot. It's an ostrich.

Arrr!

Avast, how do you like me new parrot?

That's not a parrot. It's a kangaroo.

Arrr!

Avast, how do you like me new parrot?

That's not a parrot. It's a zebra.

Arrr!

Avast, how do you like me new parrot?

That's not a parrot. It's a giraffe.

Arrr!

Avast, how do you like me new parrot?

That's not a parrot. It's an elephant.

Arrr!

8

This be the worst pet store me ever seen.

This isn't a pet store. It's a zoo.

ARRR!

9

HEARS THE THENG ABOWT SPELING TESTS

Know won kneads thim! Wee spind eviry weak studeeing four know raisin. Havunt teechairs herd uv spill chek.

I meen, hullo!

Speling tests arr such a waist uv thyme. Espeshirley sense I kan allreddy spel so guud.

FANTESTIK!

X1. AM
X2.
X3.
X4. Allrite
X5. SuPrize
X6. Potatoe

PET SPINOSAURUS

What if I had a pet spinosaurus? He'd be big and scary with sharp teeth and a loud roar.

He'd probably try to eat my Aunt Rita, which would be kind of bad, because I'd get in trouble.

Then I'd have to spend all of my money on keeping plenty of dinosaur food around so it wouldn't also try to eat my sister.

"No! Bad Spino. Spit Becky out."

SPIT. SPLECK. BLONK.

"Good, Spino. And bad, Becky. Stay out of my room next time."

I'd want him to sleep on the end of my bed at night. I guess that would break the bed.

So we'd have a slumber party on the floor. His snoring and lizard breath would make it hard to sleep.

He'd probably have a dream about chasing alligators and accidentally eat my leg off.

I'd wake up and be like, "No! Bad, Spino. Spit that out." Then I'd be late for school because the emergency room would take too long sewing my leg back on.

Okay. Maybe I don't want a pet spinosaurus.

What if I had a pet megalodon?

OLD DOG, NEW TRICK

Leroy decided to teach Old Dog a new trick.

"Old Dog, fetch." Leroy threw a stick.

Old Dog barked and ran toward the stick.

But he brought back a ball.

"No, Old Dog. The stick." Leroy tried again. "Old Dog, fetch."

Old Dog barked and ran after the stick.

But he brought back a rock.

"No, Old Dog. I threw a stick." Leroy tried again. "Old Dog, fetch."

Old Dog barked and ran after the stick.

But he brought back a bat.

"No, Old Dog. Not a bat." Leroy tried again. "Old Dog, fetch."

Old Dog barked and ran after the stick.

But he brought back a mailbox.

"No, Old Dog. Put that down." Leroy tried again. "Old Dog, fetch."

Old Dog barked and ran after the stick.

But he brought back a stop sign.

"No, Old Dog. That's not even close. Let me show you."

Leroy threw the stick again, but this time the boy wuff-wuffed like a dog and crawled after it. "See, grab it in your mouth... *wike thif.*"

Old Dog looked at the cat and smiled.

"I told you I could get our boy to fetch the stick."

BATHROOM BREAK

Oh my goodness, I guess an author shouldn't gulp down a whole sports drink while writing.
I'll be right back.

Illustrator, take over for me on this page...

Okay, I'm back.
Wait.
Illustrator, what's the deal with all of
the broken toilets?

Well, I know the title is BATHROOM BREAK.
Broken toilets is not
what that means!

19

WHAT IF UGLY DUCKLING

What if the ugly duckling's egg wasn't from a swan but from a dinosaur?

All of the other ducklings would be like, "Dude, you look like the ugliest duckling ever."

And the ugly dinosaur duckling would be like, "Dudes, you look like the yummiest ducklings ever."

And the other ducklings would say, "Oh, sorry. We were just kidding, you handsome duckling, you. Here, have some broccoli."

And they'd all live happily together forever.

OLD DOG, HOT DOG

Old Dog climbed up onto the picnic table without asking.

Leroy said, "Get down right now. You need a bath."

Old Dog stared at him. And his hot dog.

"Bad dog. Get down," said Leroy. "Go eat your dog food. You can't have mine."

Leroy held his hot dog out of reach and tried to ignore Old Dog.

Old Dog said, "Seriously, you're just going to eat that hot dog right in front of me?"

Leroy flinched. "Whoa, you can talk?" Then, he looked around and shook his head. "Whoever did that, very funny. You got me, come on out."

Old Dog scoffed. "This is no joke. I just can't handle it anymore. You can't eat hot dogs right in front of me like this."

"Why not?" Leroy asked, still looking around as if someone was pranking him.

"Are you serious? It's a hot DOG! Why don't you just chew on my leg for a while? Or here, bite my tail off. I'll get you some mustard and relish."

Leroy looked at the hot dog in his hand. "But they aren't made out of dogs. They're just called that. For some reason."

"Oh. Really? What are they made out of?"

"Um, I'd have to ask my dad. Wait, I think beef."

"Beef. I've never heard of that animal."

"Yeah, me either. I don't really like to think about the animal I'm eating anyway."

"So you pretend it's a dog instead. Are you sure beef isn't just a code name for cooked canine? Or barbecued bowwows? Or poached puppy?"

"No, of course not, it's named that for no reason. I think. Maybe."

"What if I called dog food YUMMY BOY? Mmm, I sure could chow down on some YUMMY BOY right now. How does that sound?"

"Scary. Very scary." Leroy set his hot dog down on the table. "You're right, I'm sorry. I'll go ask my dad what beef is. I'm telling you it isn't cooked dog." Leroy dashed away into the house.

Old Dog grinned.

"That was easy." Then, he gobbled up the delicious hot dog. "Yum."

LOOK MOM NO HANDS

"Look, Mom. No hands!" Clarence shouted as he zoomed around the go-kart track. He beamed his best smile as he motored past Mom.

She wasn't looking.

He waved his arms over his head.

She still stared down at her phone.

"Mom, look!" He stared backwards as his go-kart careened off the track. Mom finally looked up.

"See! No hands!" Clarence waved his arms again.

Mom's eyes flashed huge. "Look out!"

The go-kart smashed into the guard rail.

Clarence's body flung forward, and he heard a pop-pop sound as he busted through the shoulder straps and flew up and out of the go-kart.

His body twisted in midair, and he caught a glimpse of Mom both panicking and aiming her phone at him.

He waved again. "Look, Mom. No hands!"

But there was nothing to wave. His hands had gotten caught in the straps and popped off as he flew out of the go-kart.

It was so true now. No hands.

Fortunately, he had some superglue in his pocket. So after he hit the tree, bounced off the wall, and landed on the ground, the go-kart guy was able to glue his hands back on.

Clarence wiggled his fingers and sighed.

"Phew, I'm glad I had that superglue in my pocket. It sure came in handy."

Cowboy Robot

Have you ever read the story about the cowboy who was actually a robot, but wanted to be a ninja until the day he got bitten by an alien werewolf pirate?

I haven't either, but it sounds cool.

I wish I knew an author who could write something like that.

But I don't.

Oh well.

The end.

THE BEST COW TIPPING EVER

*T*wo cows stood at the edge of a field under the stars.

"Hey. Here comes another couple of kids," the first cow said.

"Cow-tippers again? Humans are so odd," said cow number two.

"Yeah, but at least it adds a little fun to our night. Remember those last kids we chased away, and the one got stuck in the fence."

"Hee, hee," the second cow chuckled. "That was fun. Let's do that again."

"No, hold on. I have a new idea," said the first cow. "Go hide behind that tree and watch. This is gonna be great."

Missy snuck under the fence and held up the wire
so her cousin Bernie could follow.

"Cow tipping. This is gonna be great," Missy
whispered.

"I still don't understand," said Bernie. "It sounds
dangerous and not much fun."

"You poor city boy." She shined her flashlight right
in his eyes. "Cow tipping is funner than anything you've
ever done before. I promise."

They walked through the dark field with crickets
chirping all around. An owl hooted from the trees
nearby. Bernie flinched and bumped into Missy.

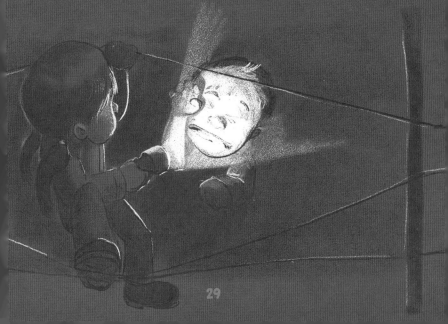

"Whoa! Watch it, Bernie," Missy said. "It isn't called cousin tipping. I almost fell on that cowpie."

"Cowpie? You mean that pile of poop. Gross. Why do you call it pie?"

"Uh, I don't know. I'm not a poop-namer. You've really never heard of cowpies?" Missy asked.

"Missy, I've never even seen a cow up close. Let alone its pies. Oh gross. It is icky just saying that out loud. I might never eat chocolate pie again."

"Shh!" Missy stopped and clicked off the flashlight. "Cow just ahead. See it standing there sleeping?" she whispered.

"Sleeping? Standing up? Shouldn't it be lying down?" Bernie asked.

"Of course not. How would we tip it over if it was sleeping on the ground?"

"Do I really have to do this? It seems mean."

Missy put her arm around Bernie's shoulders. "If you don't have a heap of fun, I'll eat a cowpie sandwich."

"Ohhh-kay. That's gross and doesn't make me feel better," Bernie said. "Can I just watch you this time? On the first one."

"Fine. I'll tiptoe closer now. You watch how I do it." Missy's smile shined in the moonlight. "I mean, I've never done this before either, but I've heard all about it."

Bernie threw up his hands. "What? You've never cow tipped either? Why did I follow you out here?"

"Good grief," Missy whispered. "It isn't rocket science. I just sneak up there, give that cow a big ole push, and it falls over. And then, we high-five and laugh really hard."

"Whatever," Bernie whispered. "Let's get it over with."

Missy beamed. "Now you're talking. Watch and learn, City Boy. Here comes the best cow tipping ever."

Missy led the way forward, tiptoeing closer and closer toward the sleeping cow. Bernie stopped a few feet away as Missy stepped right up to the cow's side. The animal was big and fat and smelled like mud and poop. She could hear it snoring a little bit.

Missy giggled to herself as she reared back her arms and then shoved the cow's stomach.

"Oof." Nothing happened. She felt like she'd pushed on a fuzzy wall.

Missy widened her stance and squatted low. She heaved again.

"Oof." The cow didn't budge and kept on snoring.

"Holy hefty cow," Missy mumbled to herself. "She squatted even lower and pressed her shoulder against the cow's belly.

"Ooof!" She pushed off with her legs and the fuzzy wall of belly finally tilted. The cow swayed, but only about an inch. And then more snoring.

Missy whisper-hissed over to Bernie. "Hey, get over here. I almost got it, but I need your help."

Bernie stood and watched for a long moment.

"Fun or a cowpie sandwich," Missy promised.

"Still gross, but fine," Bernie mumbled. He tiptoed over.

"Squat down like I am. Put your shoulder into it and push with your legs. Like this."

Bernie knelt down halfheartedly and leaned into the furry wall of cow belly.

"It smells like my cat's bottom!"

"Focus," Missy whispered. "I'll count to three and then we shove. Okay?"

"Okay." Bernie sounded miserable.

"This is going to be so great," Missy giggled. "Okay. Here we go. I Mississippi. 2 Mississippi. And—"

*T*he first cow flashed open her eyes.

"MOO! HaHa!" The animal leaned to the side and body slammed itself over, right on top of the kids.

The kids groaned as they lay flattened into a cowpie sandwich between the cow and two piles of poop.

"Hee, hee!" the cow mooed again. She jumped up and jogged over to the second cow who'd been watching from behind the tree.

"Did you see that? I got both of them in one shot. I just invented *kid crushing*. Best thing ever!"

They clapped a high-hoof and laughed really hard as the kids got up and stumbled away.

WHAT IF CINDERELLA

What if instead of a fairy godmother, Cinderella was visited by a granddaddy longlegs? I bet that would have been boring.

The end.

BATHROOM BREAK AGAIN

Sorry.
These sports drinks go right through me.
Illustrator, take over again.
No broken toilets this time...

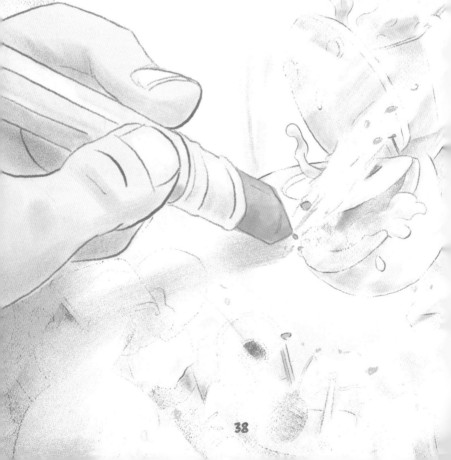

Phew, I barely made it to the bathroom.
Wait.
Illustrator, toilets again? Seriously?

Yeah, I see they aren't broken this time.
I meant that you could
draw anything in the world.
Not just toilets.

You're so weird.

THE BEST THING ABOUT BEING A KNIGHT

PART 1

The best thing about being a knight in this day and age is that there are no more dragons. My whole life is like a big vacation.

Take today for instance. Here's my schedule:

8am- Breakfast with Prince Genzo

9am- Video games with Princess Nanako

10:30am- Brunch with Queen Runa

11:15am- Ride my bike over to say hello to my former horse at his new home

11:45am- Shine armor (that I only wear on Halloween)

11:55am- Take a nap

12:30pm- Take private jet to beach for lunch and swimming with Princes and Princesses

2pm- Nerf sword practice with Princess Maki

2:30pm- Take another na—

KNOCK, KNOCK!

Hold on, there's somebody at my door.

"Who is it?"

"A servant, Sir. I have an urgent message for Sir Ed, Bravest of Brave Knight of the 21st Century."

"Well, that's me. Come on in."

"Thank you, Sir. I have an urgent message from—"

"Would you like a donut?"

"No. Uh, thank you, Sir. As I was saying, an urgent mess—"

"Are you sure? They have rainbow sprinkles on them, and I'm about to go have breakfast with Prince Genzo. I do hate wasting donuts."

"Well, perhaps one donut. Thank you, Sir. You are very kind."

"So you were saying. An urgent message. Is brunch canceled?"

"Naw, Sir. Thar wuz a dwahgon spotted..."

"Good grief, Messenger. Don't talk with your mouth full of donut. Have you no manners?"

Gulp. "Sorry, Sir. Sorry. I was saying. There was a—"

"Here, use a napkin. You've got icing and sprinkles stuck to your chin."

"Oh, terribly sorry, Sir."

"Yes, there you go. You got it. Now, enough of this babbling. Spit out the message. What was it you were saying? Brunch canceled?"

"No Sir. Well, yes sir. I should think so. But it is about a dragon, Sir. A dragon has flown from the volcano north of the castle."

"A dragon? Ha, funny joke. There is not even a volcano north of the castle. Did Princess Runa put you up to this?"

"Not a joke, Sir. There is now a volcano. It just popped up overnight. I saw it myself from the castle wall. The Queen has sent for you as the dragon has already burned down the mall and the movie theater in the northern suburban kingdom."

"The movie theater? What a monster!"

"Indeed, Sir. Are you feeling okay?"

"As a matter of fact, I am not. Woke up a little feverish. A lot feverish. Here, feel my forehead."

"Seems normal, Sir.

"Oh, so now you're a doctor are you?"

"No, Sir. Only a messenger, Sir."

"And don't you forget it. Next thing we know, you'll be telling me how to slay a dragon."

"Of course not, Sir. You're the expert, Sir."

"No, seriously, Messenger. I'm really asking, how would you kill the dragon? I've no idea. They were supposed to be extinct. Perhaps even fairy tales to begin with. How could a volcano sprout like a beanstalk and burp forth a beast like this? I'm going to die, Messenger. A horrific fiery death. My funeral will smell like burnt popcorn overcooked in the microwave."

"Um, well, uh, this is awkward, Sir."

"Well, of course, it is. There's a winged, fire-breathing dinosaur out there. Awkward is an understatement."

"Yes, Sir. I see. But, you were born for this. From a long line of heroic knights. I have three sets of your kingdom cards. Mint condition. You've trained for this your whole life, Sir."

"With video games and foam swords! It hasn't ever been serious. Picture it, Messenger. Walking up the street and facing off against a twelve-foot, fiery beast."

"I hear it is more like twenty feet, Sir."

"Twenty feet tall? I'm sick. Seriously. Call the Queen. I'm going to be absent today."

"Sir. I think you can do this. I'll help you. Let's put your armor on and you'll feel more like your title, Sir Ed, Bravest of Brave Knight of the 21st Century. And your sword. Where is your sword?"

"I traded it online for Pokémon cards."

"Sir, you didn't!"

"I did. Why would I need a real sword? Do you know how sharp that thing was? You don't just keep a double-edged, giant knife lying around your house, do you?"

"Then, your armor, Sir. Let's focus on your armor."

"It's too heavy. And uncomfortable. And if the dragon breathes on me it'll heat up like a frying pan and cook me inside. I mean, seriously. Armor against a dragon is kind of stupid if you stop and think about it."

"But, Sir, if you don't slay the dragon the castle will be destroyed."

"Yes, but it is like a thousand years old. Time for a new castle anyway, don't you think?"

"Sir, no longer will they call you Bravest of Brave Knight of the 21st Century. Your legacy will be gone."

"Oh, my legacy. I didn't think of that. Also, no more special parking spot, and I'd lose my 10% discount at the gift shop.

"Messenger, you are right. Forgive me for stalling. I am Sir Ed, the Bravest of Brave Knight. I shall answer this call to action. I will fight the dragon!"

"Oh, Sir! How magnificent of you. Come along, right this way."

"No, hold on. First, I have to figure out a replacement sword. Maybe I have something in the kitchen.

"Here's a spatula."

"Sir. I don't think a spatula will work."

"This butter knife is a mini-sword."

"Uh, Sir. That's probably inadequate for the job."

"Fine. I'll order a sword online. Let's see. Where did I put my phone? Here it is.

"Oooh, cool. This one has a Yoshi on the hilt. And it's available for one-day shipping. *Click*. And ordered."

"Brilliant choice, Sir. I guess."

"Thank you. Now leave at once. Tell the Queen that I, Sir Ed, Bravest of Brave Knight of the 21st Century, shall launch an urgent quest to slay the dragon.

"Tomorrow. After the mail gets here."

WHAT IF PINOCCHIO

What if it was Pinocchio's arm muscles that grew
when he lied? He'd be a huge muscle-puppet.
And when somebody called him a puppet, he'd pound
them on the head until they agreed he was a boy.
But of course, he'd still be a puppet.

POUND

Ow, my head!
Pinocchio, how did you get out of my story?
Get back in there you silly puppet.

POUND

Ow. Okay, you're a boy. Ouch.

(Psst. Reader. Help!
There's an angry, muscle-puppet
in my office!)

POUND.

Ow! I mean, muscle-boy.
Quit pounding my head, Pinocchio.

The end.

(Sheesh.)

GOODNIGHT BUGS

In the great outdoors
Near a campfire,
There was a boy
And his family
Settling down for bedtime.

Goodnight fireflies
Goodnight bees
Goodnight cicadas in the trees

Goodnight roaches
Goodnight gnats
Goodnight mosquitoes dodging slaps

Goodnight moth. Do your dance
Goodnight cricket in Dad's pants

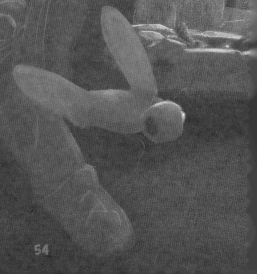

Goodnight wasp up in the air
Goodnight spider in Mom's hair

Goodnight mantis
Goodnight tick
Goodnight scorpion
And walking stick

Goodnight bugs near and far...

I guess I'm sleeping in the car.

PERIOD

Once upon a time, there was a period

who was so pumped to finish

the sentence that the sentence

grew too exciting

for him in the

end!

Hey, no fair.

Then another sentence was written,

but this time, the sentence turned

into a— guess

what?

EGHHH

Quit stealing my spots.

10 Things to do After a Werewolf Bites Your Leg

Picture this. You're walking along the sidewalk, minding your own business, when CRUNCH a werewolf bites your leg, howls with laughter, and then runs away.

First of all, what in the world were you doing walking along the sidewalk under a full moon? I thought you were smarter than that.

Second, you're now officially sick with *lunar-howler-furry-osis*, which is fancy, doctor-talk for: the next full moon will turn you into a werewolf. There's nothing you can do to stop it.

However, you can make the best of it by being prepared.

Here is a list of things to do...

10 THINGS TO DO AFTER A WEREWOLF BITES YOUR LEG

1. Finish your walk along the sidewalk because it is the last time you will see a full moon through the eyes of a non-wolfy kid.

(While walking, don't let a vampire bite you. Sharing your new werewolf blood with a poor, unsuspecting bat-person is rude.)

2. Practice howling at the sky and ceiling as much as possible. There's nothing more embarrassing than being a bad howler.

(If your mom, bus driver, or teacher tells you to stop, simply explain your lunar-howler-furry-osis situation, and I'm sure they'll understand.)

3. Pick out a good veterinarian and get shots to make sure the werewolf didn't also give you a cold. Howling with a runny nose produces super silly and embarrassing sounds.

4. Ask your dog about his favorite kind of dog food and biscuits. You will build up a huge appetite running around on full moon nights, so be ready with his delicious suggestions.

5. Begin staying up all night and sleeping all day. The other werewolves are wonderful pranksters, and if you are caught sleeping on a full moon night, you'll probably wake up with your fur shaved off and a mustache drawn on your face with a marker.

(If your mom, bus driver, or teacher tells you to stop day-sleeping, simply explain your lunar-howler-furry-osis situation, and I'm sure they'll understand.)

6. Do an internet search for anyone in your neighborhood with the last name *Ridinghood*. Then plan to stay far away from their property. This family has spread vicious rumors about wolfkind for centuries.

7. Tattoo a map of the area onto your palm. Werewolves are always getting lost and losing things. Having a tattoo map on the furless part of your hand keeps your werewolf-self from having to ask for directions.

8. Pack about fifteen backpacks of extra clothes and hide them all around the woods and your town. Your furry, werewolf self won't need the clothes, but when the full moon sets and your fur disappears, you'll want one of those backpacks to be close by.

9. List all of your best friends on a piece of paper and make sure you know how to run to their house. You will want to bite them on the leg as soon as possible so that you can have full moon playdates. (*You may need to trick your friends into thinking that sidewalk walks under a full moon are a great and smart thing.*)

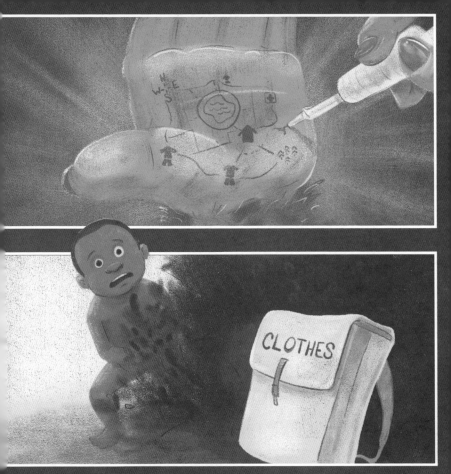

10. Stop bringing your school work home because when your new canine genes kick in, you'll start eating all of your homework. I mean, why waste your time, when you can eat your little brother's homework instead?

(If your mom, teacher, or little brother complains, simply explain your lunar-howler-furry-osis situation, and I'm sure they'll understand.)

YET ANOTHER BATHROOM BREAK

I'm sorry.
I tried to wait, but I can't!

Illustrator, use your imagination.
This time don't draw a bunch of toilets.

Okay, I'm back. Sorry about that.

Illustrator, I said no toilets!

Oh come on,
"don't draw a bunch of toilets" didn't mean
draw one toilet.
Dude, your toilet obsession is so strange.

WHAT IF JACK AND JILL

What if Jack just orders the dangerous hill bulldozed down to a flat spot. I mean, if he has a crown that can break, he's got to be a prince with all kinds of money and gold, right? Once the hill is bulldozed, the water is on level ground. Clumsy Prince Jack might fall down and say, "Ouch. My crown." But at least he won't break it tumbling from way up on the hill.

Or, why doesn't Prince Jack just have one of his servants fetch the water? I mean, what prince has ever fetched his own water from up a scary, tumbly hill?

And why are they fetching water with a pail? Hello, a garden hose!

Or are they camping? But who takes a crown on a camping trip in the first place? I'm starting to think Prince Jack is just not very smart.

And this Jill character. She watches Jack tumble down the hill and is like, "Oh fun, my turn!"

That girl has no sense either.

SILLY ANSWERS TO SOLID QUESTIONS

Question:
Why is the sky blue?

Answer:
Actually, the sky isn't blue.
It is orange with purple polka dots.
But astronauts like blue better,
so they spray paint the sky every morning.

BLUE

Beautiful work, Baby.

Question:
Which came first, the chicken or the egg?

Answer:
The chicken came first, which I know because
I looked it up in the dictionary.

C before E,
Baby.

Question:
If you could time travel, where would you go?

Answer:
Breakfast.

Double waffles
today, Baby.

Question:

If you could have a superpower, what would it be?

Answer:

Fruit punch out of the nose.

Villains beware, Baby.

Question:

If a genie gave you three wishes, what would they be?

Answer:

Waffles.

1 waffle. 2 waffles. 3 waffles, Baby.

Question:

If you could have any animal as a pet, what would it be?

Answer:

A big-beaked, screaming-scramming, chicken-chicken.

Best alarm clock ever, Baby.

Question:

How many more random questions can an author think up before he has to run to the bathroom again?

Answer:

One and a half.

I can see the future, Baby.

Question:
If you were stranded on a deserted island, what would be the one thing you'd want to have?

Answer:
A chocolate brownie sundae with fruit punch flavored sprinkles in a waffle cone bowl.

Sweetest *desserted* island ever, Baby.

Question:
If you could choose between an unending summer vacation or a big giant--

Uh oh! Gotta stop this story!!!

BATHROOM BREAK EMERGENCY!

I can't hold it!
Illustrator, this time
don't you dare draw toilets.
Oh, nevermind.
Draw whatever.
I've gotta run for it...

Whew. Made it.
Sorry I ran off like that.

Illustrator, what a surprise.
More toilet art.

Oh, I get it,
"BATHROOM BREAK EMERGENCY".
I actually grinned a little at that one.
You're still weird though.

Very, very weird.

A NINJA NUNCHUCKED MY NOTEBOOK

NICE JOB!

You'd be so proud, Ms. T.

I had my research article written. You would have given me two smiley face stickers. Guaranteed.

But here's the thing. My notebook is gone. All gone! And it's not even my fault.

Because last night, my notebook was attacked...

By a ninja!

I agree, Ms. T., it sounds totally farfetched. Like a BIG ole lie. I know, I know. But honest.

A ninja nunchucked my notebook!

Here's what happened. I had just finished the entire assignment and was guarding it from my hungry dog, Gus, because you know what happened last week. Suddenly, I noticed the window open in my room.

At first, I thought it was Gus trying to distract me. But then, I remembered something super important. Gus has paws, not hands. Paws can't lift windows. Hands do!

Which is when I remembered who has hands...

A ninja!

A hiding, sneaking ninja who was after my notebook!

Why would a ninja want my notebook?

That's a great question, and I have the answer.

Here. Lean closer, and I'll tell you.

It's because of what I had chosen as my research topic.
TOP SECRET NINJA SECRETS.
Shhh.
Don't tell anybody.
It's too dangerous.
I know that now, Ms. T., and I wouldn't want you to get hurt.

Okay, back to last night. I looked around my bedroom, and of course, I couldn't see the ninja, but still, I hurry-up lunged for my notebook.

"Back off, Ninja!" I shouted. "I will turn this into my teacher tomorrow or go to the hospital trying." That's right, Ms. T., I care about my education that much, despite having no chance against a trained, combat ninja.

Still, I planted my feet on the carpet, and I hugged my notebook with a death grip so tight it would have taken ten ninjas to pry it loose. Ten normal, combat ninjas, that is.

Little did I know that this was no normal ninja I was dealing with. Because right then, *ker-swish*, this ninja double backflipped in out of nowhere and landed right in front of me.

But then, when I was bracing for a ninja-chop to my face, the ninja reached out and tickled me.

Yeah, tickled me!

I mean, Ms. T., who has ever heard of a Tickle Ninja?

~TICKLE~
~TICKLE~
~TICKLE~

Well, I know that sounds ridiculous, Ms. T., but it is actually brilliant once you think about it. Renders a person useless without leaving a mark. I mean, if he'd *kiya'ed* me between the eyes, and I dropped the notebook, at least I could have shown you my beat-up face. But do you know how silly I feel telling you I dropped my notebook on the floor because of ninja tickle torture?

I wasn't ready for that. I laughed and wriggled, and as soon as my notebook dropped, *swish-swish SMACK*, the ninja nunchucked my notebook right out the window.

Then, he *flip-twist-leaped* out, caught my notebook in midair, somersaulted into a soft landing, and vanished behind the tree in my neighbor's yard.

Yes, I know this is unbelievable, Ms. T. All of those top-secret ninja secrets lost. And I can't even add the newly experienced *Tickle Ninja Tickle Torture* to the list.

Oh my goodness, Ms. T. Can you stink'n believe it?

A ninja going around nunchucking notebooks!

Ms. T., I'm not trying to blame anyone, but you should be more careful with your homework assignments. Might want to skip them for a few weeks while this all blows over.

Homework. Such a dangerous endeavor.

HOW TO SCARE THINGS

How to scare a rock.

HOW TO SCARE A BLADE OF GRASS.

HOW TO SCARE A FLOWER.

HOW TO SCARE A KID!

The Best Thing About Being A Knight

Part 2- The Next Day

The best thing about being a knight is nothing.

At least not now that dragons are real again, and I have to wear this ridiculously heavy armor *slash* knight-oven that will cook me like a baked potato when the dragon breathes on me.

Or I might have a heart attack first, hiking up this hill to find the thing. Oh my goodness, I shouldn't have traded my horse for a ping pong table last week. It seemed like a good deal at the time, but I'd give up three ping pong tables to be riding on a horse right now.

Here let me sit for a minute and catch my breath.

Ugh. Let me take off this helmet.

Phew. That's better. Fresh air.

Oh, crud!

My helmet is rolling. Gotta get up. Fast.

Erg— gotta grab it—*oog* —before it rolls down the—

eeg —hill.

Dang, this armor!

Forget getting up fast. I can't get up at all.

And there goes my helmet bouncing off the trail.

Bounce-bounce.

And over the cliff.

Bye-bye helmet. I hated you anyway, but my face will

probably miss you come dragon time.

Oh well, I'll just rest here a while until I have the

strength to get up.

Oh man, what if I can't get up later either. I'll have to call mountain rescue to help me stand up. That'll be so embarrassing.

Though I'm not sure if I'll get a signal up here to call them. Better check my phone.

Okay, yeah I have one bar. *Phew.*

Oh, and a notification that a Pokémon Go egg hatched. Nice. My dragon hike paid off already.

Wait.

What's that sound? That stomping, crashing sound.

It's getting closer. Oh, and now a roar.

I should hide. *Erg—eeg—oog.* Oh yeah, I can't get up.

Maybe I can lean onto my side—*clunk*—and roll under that bush on the other side of the trail—*clink-clank, clink-clank, CLUNK.*

Stupid rock is in the way.

"Roarrr!"

Oh my goodness, it's gotta be the dragon. And just around the next bend.

The stomping feels like an earthquake!

Oh, crud. Rolling away from the tree was a bad idea.
Now I am laying in the middle of the trail, ready to get
burned up like a human hot dog.

Well, maybe he'll mistake me for a log. Would a
dragon know the difference? I'll think loggy thoughts. *I
am made of wood.* Wait! Wood burns. Like really, really
burns. I'm a goner!

"Grr, metal log trip me. Probably scary knight put it
there.

"Oh no, must be scary knight trap. He be close by. I
fly now. No, he see me. I hide now. Yeah, hide. But where
hide?

"I know! Under metal log. He never find me."

"Grr, why metal log have boots?"

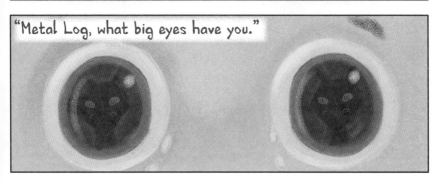

"Metal Log, what big eyes have you."

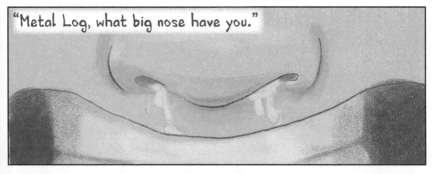

"Metal Log, what big nose have you."

"Metal Log, are you Big Bad Wolf?"

"Um, yes. Yes. You are right. I'm the Big Bad Wolf. Ha. You caught me."

"So glad you not scary knight."

"Ha-ha. No scary knight here. I promise you that."

"Okay, Big Bad Wolf. I burn you up now."

"Burn me up! But, I'm not the scary knight."

"Me know, but you big meanie to Little Red and nice three pigs. I know stories. Goodbye."

"No, wait. I was joking. Ha. Got you. I'm not the Big Bad Wolf at all. I'm the, um, scary knight. My, uh, trap worked."

"Nice try, Mr. Wolf. Bye, bye again."

"Wait. Look. I'm not furry. And this thing is where my sword goes and this is armor. I'm a knight."

"Gasp. You are knight! Oh no!"

"Yes, I am Sir Ed, Bravest of Brave Knight."

"Hold horses. You knight, but you not scary like Sir Ed."

"Yeah, I am. I'm totally him. Honest."

"No way you him. I have Sir Ed Kingdom Cards and you not him at all."

"Seriously, I am him. Here, this is the pose on my Rookie Legend card."

"You not him. Ed has sword, not butter knife."

"Yes, okay. My sword is gone. I ordered a new one but the next-day delivery was late."

"Grr, me hate late delivery. Kingdom Cards late two days last time. Still, Ed have helmet. You none."

"My helmet bounced off the cliff right before you got here."

"Oh, that not good for knight. I burn face off with fire-breath. Now I believe you be Sir Ed, but you not scary like cards and stories."

"You're right. I'm not that scary, or brave, to be honest. They sent me up here to slay you because you burned down the mall. But, maybe we could clear all of this up if you apologize."

"Me am sorry. Allergy season. Me fly over mall and sneeze. Accident."

"So, you weren't attacking the kingdom?"

"No way. I hide always with friends unicorn and Loch Ness monster. No fun fighting scary knights."

"Well, we're on the same page then. I won't slay you if you don't burn me to a crisp. Deal?"

"Yes, me deal."

"You're pretty cool, Dragon. It was nice meeting you."

"Nice meet you, Ed."

"Hey, Dragon. Before you go. Could you help me stand up? This armor is ridiculously heavy."

"Sure. Not problem. Me agree armor ridiculous. Protect outside from fire breath but inside make you baked potato."

"That's what I said! I think I'll trade it in when I get back to the castle. I wonder what I can get for armor with a missing helmet."

"Before leave, you sign me Sir Ed Kingdom Cards?"

"Sure buddy. No problem."

EVERYTHING IS BETTER WITH NINJAS

School?

With ninjas!

Lunch?

With ninjas!

Presidents?

With ninjas!

- EVERYTHING IS BETTER WITH NINJAS! -

THE END

THE END

(WITH NINJAS!)

ABOUT THE AUTHOR
(with ninjas!)

Through the foggy mist of twilight, Michael Wayne first appeared near the village of St. James, MO. He grew fierce in the sacred art of story nunchucking at Chatham University. He is credited with training the legendary Snowman Ninja, of SNOWMAN VS. picture book lore.

Michael lurks in the forests and prairies outside of Chicago, Illinois, accompanied by a lovely ninja, a young ninja, and a young dragon.

To learn more, backflip over to michaelwaynebooks.com.

ABOUT THE ILLUSTRATOR
(with ninjas!)

He's Jeremy Manning.

Master of shadows. Shaper of color and art.

KIYA! University of Central Missouri. BFA. Did it.

KIYA! Designer. Plein-air painter. Illustrator. Does it.

KIYA! First children's book. Doing it.

KIYA! Kansas City, MO. Wife. Two daughters. Dogs. Loving it.

KIYA! Jeremymanning.com. Visit it.

KIYA!